This book
_____

A catalogue record for this book is available from the British Library

Published by Ladybird Books Ltd
80 Strand, London, WC2R 0RL
A Penguin Company

2 4 6 8 10 9 7 5 3 1
© LADYBIRD BOOKS LTD MMVIII
LADYBIRD and the device of a Ladybird are trademarks of Ladybird Books Ltd

ISBN: 978-1-84646-940-4
Printed in China

My Storytime

Sam Tractor to the Rescue

written by Nicola Baxter
illustrated by Alex Burnett

Farmer Fred scratched his head.

"It's going to snow and it's going to blow," he said, "or I'm a turnip. All the animals must come into the barn."

So Sam Tractor and his trailer trundled off across the farm to find the pigs.

The pigs were in the pen, snuffling and munching.

"You must come into the barn," said Sam Tractor. "Farmer Fred thinks it's going to snow."

"Snow?" grunted the greedy pigs. "How does he know it's going to snow? We're staying right here... *snuffle*... with these... *munch*... tasty turnip tops, thank you very much."

So off trundled Sam Tractor to find the cows.

The cows were in the meadow, chewing and mooing.

"You must come into the barn," said Sam Tractor. "Farmer Fred says it's going to snow."

"*Oooh, nooo,*" the cows mooed slowly. "A little bit of *snooow* doesn't worry us, you *knooow.* We're not… *chew…* leaving this… *chew… juuuicy* green grass, thank you very much."

So off trundled Sam Tractor to find the hens.

The hens were in the yard, pecking and scratching.

"You must come into the barn," said Sam Tractor. "Farmer Fred is sure it's going to snow."

Sam

"Snow? What's that?" clucked the hens nervously. "Now we're all of a twitter. Don't come bothering us… *cluck*… with silly… *cluck*… stories, thank you very much."

So off trundled Sam Tractor to find the ducks.

The ducks were in the pond, dipping and diving.

"You must come into the barn," said Sam Tractor. "Farmer Fred is certain it's going to snow."

"Is that a fact?" quacked the dabbling ducks. "We're not worried by a little bit of wind and wet. We're… *quack*… happy… *quack*… whatever the weather, thank you very much."

So off trundled Sam Tractor to find the sheep.

The sheep were on the hillside huddled together.

"You must come into the barn," said Sam Tractor. "Farmer Fred knows it's going to snow."

"The *baaarn*?" bleated the sheep.
"You must be *baaarmy*. Our woolly coats
are the warmest on the *faaarm*, thank you
very much."

So off trundled Sam Tractor to find
the horse.

The horse was in the paddock, lazily leaning on the gate.

"You must come into the barn," said Sam Tractor. "Farmer Fred is as sure as he can be that it's going to snow."

"*Todaaay?*" neighed the horse with a yawn. "Oh, what a bore. I'd rather *staaay*, old chap, thank you very much."

So off trundled Sam Tractor back to the farmhouse.

Farmer Fred just stood and scratched his head again.

"If those uppity animals won't come," he said, "they can stay where they are. You can go into the barn."

He went back into the warm farmhouse
and banged the door shut.

As Sam Tractor trundled across
the yard, the first fluffy flakes of snow
began to fall.

Sam Tractor looked out from the barn.
On the farm everything was white and
whirling.

"It's snowing and blowing all right," he
thought. "Oh bother! I can't stay here.
I'm going to have to bring those uppity
animals into the barn."

So off trundled Sam Tractor. The snow was cool and crunchy and icy wind whistled round his wheels.

Sam Tractor came to the pig pen. "Come on pigs, you can bring those turnip tops with you," he said. And the pigs climbed into the trailer without a grunt or a grumble.

Sam Tractor came to the meadow. "Come on cows, your grass isn't so green now!" he said. And the cows climbed into the trailer without a moo or a moan.

Sam Tractor came to the yard. "Come on hens, before your beaks turn blue!" he said. And the hens fluttered on board without a twitter or a cluck.

Sam Tractor came to the pond. It was frozen solid. "Come on, you daft ducks," he said. And the ducks slid across the ice without a single quack.

Sam Tractor came to the hillside. Even the sheep were shivering.

"Come on, there's room for all of you,"
said Sam Tractor kindly. And they shuffled
on board without a baa or a bleat.

Sam Tractor came to the paddock.
"Come on horse, follow us!" he cried.
And the horse lolloped quietly behind
him all the way back to the barn.

All night long, it was snowing and blowing.
But Sam Tractor and the pigs and the
cows and the hens and the ducks and
the sheep and the horse were safe in
the barn.

Sam

And with a *grunt* and a *moo* and a *cluck*
and a *quack* and a *baa* and a *neigh*,
all those uppity animals turned to say,
"Sam Tractor, thank you very much!"